CORDUROY
LOST AND FOUND

Story by B. G. Hennessy
Pictures by Jody Wheeler
Based on the character created by Don Freeman

SCHOLASTIC INC.
New York Toronto London Auckland Sydney
Mexico City New Delhi Hong Kong Buenos Aires

For Don and Lydia Freeman,
two bigger hearts you'll never find. —B.G.H.

Based on the character by Don Freeman

ISBN-13: 978-0-545-00422-0
ISBN-10: 0-545-00422-5

15 14 13 12 11 10 9 8 7 6   13 14 15 16 17 18/0
Printed in the U.S.A.

First Scholastic paperback printing, January 2008   08

Set in Cloister

One sunny Saturday afternoon, Lisa and her mother were riding the bus home from a shopping trip. Corduroy sat comfortably on Lisa's lap as the bus bumped along. She held on to him so he wouldn't fall. Lisa took very good care of Corduroy.

He looked out the window while Lisa and her mother talked about Lisa's birthday.

Corduroy's ears perked right up. "Lisa is having a birthday and I don't have a present for her!" he said to himself. He looked out the window at all the stores. "I wonder what she would like," he thought.

They all got off the bus at the next stop. Lisa's mother rode the elevator up to their apartment, but Corduroy and Lisa liked to run up the stairs two at a time to see if they could get there first.

That night Corduroy lay awake long after Lisa fell asleep. He was worried about her present. "I need to find something special," he decided.

Very early the next morning, Corduroy slipped out of bed, tiptoed out of Lisa's room, and crept through the apartment.

He opened the front door and stepped into the hallway.

Just then, the elevator doors opened. "Maybe I'll find something for Lisa in here," said Corduroy as he looked in.

Corduroy looked at the buttons on the wall. Each button had a number on it. "This is like a game!" Corduroy said. "Lisa might like a game for her birthday." Corduroy climbed up on the stool and pressed a button.

All at once, the doors closed and the elevator began to move up. "This is like a rocket ship," thought Corduroy. "Maybe Lisa would like to ride in a rocket ship for her birthday!" Corduroy pressed more buttons. Down and up, up and down he went.

Finally the elevator came to a stop. When the doors opened, Corduroy
stepped out into the lobby.

Peeking out over the roof of the building across the street, Corduroy
saw just what he was looking for.

"It's the biggest, prettiest balloon I ever saw," thought Corduroy.
"That is what I want to give Lisa for her birthday!"

Corduroy had never before been outside when it was still dark. The familiar neighborhood looked very different. And where was Lisa's balloon? Then he saw it at the end of the street. "It's getting away!" cried Corduroy. He ran as fast as he could to catch it.

Before he had gone very far, he saw a big brown dog. "Maybe Lisa would like a pet for her birthday," thought Corduroy.

"Hello," he said to the dog.

"*Arrrf,*" barked the dog, and it picked him up by the overalls and carried him down the street.

Just when they got to the corner, a big, noisy truck slowed down, and someone threw a tall stack of newspapers onto the sidewalk. The dog was so surprised that he dropped Corduroy on top of the papers.

That is where Mr. Gonzales, the owner of the newsstand, found Corduroy sitting all by himself.

"Where in the world did you come from, *mi amigo*?"

He put Corduroy up on a shelf. "I think someone must have dropped you. You look like a very special bear and I bet they will be back for you. Until then, you can help me sell my papers."

From up on the shelf, Corduroy could see everything that was going on. As people bought papers, Corduroy smiled shyly at them. "This must be a job!" said Corduroy. "I've always wanted a job!"

A woman stopped in front of the newsstand. "How much for the bear?" she asked. "Sorry, *señora*, this bear is not for sale. He is lost and is waiting to be found," said Mr. Gonzales.

LOST? Corduroy had *never* wanted to be lost! He thought about Lisa. He knew that she would be worried about him. Then Corduroy remembered the balloon. He had forgotten all about it. Where was it?

Corduroy looked up and down the street. It wasn't as dark anymore.
But he didn't see the beautiful balloon anywhere.

Now he was sad and sleepy. He wanted to be home with Lisa. Corduroy fell asleep thinking about balloons and home.

He was just waking up when he heard a familiar voice.

A very worried Lisa was asking Mr. Gonzales if she could put up a sign she made for her lost bear.

"This is a very good picture, *señorita*," said Mr. Gonzales.

"But you won't need this sign; your bear is here with me." Mr. Gonzales took Corduroy down from the shelf and gave him a lollipop. It looked just like the balloon he had wanted to give to Lisa!

"*Muchas gracias, señor,*" said Lisa.

"Thank you for helping me, Corduroy," said Mr. Gonzales. *"Adios."*

Corduroy and Lisa were so happy they ran all the way home and up the stairs, two at a time.

"Corduroy, I was so worried about you!" said Lisa. "The only thing I wanted for my birthday was to have my best friend back home with me!"

Lisa gave Corduroy a big hug.

"That's exactly what I wanted, too!" thought Corduroy, and he gave
Lisa a birthday hug right back.